**W9-DES-309**

THE TREE WITH EYES

by Hubert Ben Kemoun

illustrated by François Roca
translated by Genevieve Chamberland

Librarian Reviewer
Marci Peschke
Librarian, Dallas Independent School District
MA Education Reading Specialist, Stephen F. Austin State University
Learning Resources Endorsement, Texas Women's University

Reading Consultant
Elizabeth Stedem
Educator/Consultant, Colorado Springs, CO
MA in Elementary Education, University of Denver, CO

STONE ARCH BOOKS
MINNEAPOLIS   SAN DIEGO

First published in the United States in 2008
by Stone Arch Books,
151 Good Counsel Drive, P.O. Box 669
Mankato, Minnesota 56002
www.stonearchbooks.com

Library of Congress Cataloging-in-Publication Data
Ben Kemoun, Hubert, 1958–
   [Terriblement vert! English]
   The Tree with Eyes / by Hubert Ben Kemoun; translated by
Genevieve Chamberland; illustrated by François Roca.
      p. cm. — (Pathway Books Editions / The Adventures of Sam X)
      ISBN 978-1-4342-0481-3 (library binding)
      ISBN 978-1-4342-0531-5 (paperback)
      [1. Trees—Fiction. 2. Supernatural—Fiction.] I. Chamberland,
Genevieve. II. Roca, François, ill. III. Title.
PZ7.B4248Tr 2008
[Fic]—dc222007030800

Summary: Lionel begins to turn into a tree after eating seeds that Sam's
uncle brought from the Amazon. Sam tries to bring him to the hospital,
but when he puts Lionel next to the river for some water, Lionel becomes
planted there and the tree grows around him. Sam and his uncle must get
Lionel out of the tree.

Art Director: Heather Kindseth
Graphic Designer: Kay Fraser

1 2 3 4 5 6 13 12 11 10 09 08

Printed in the United States of America

TABLE OF CONTENTS

Chapter 1

STRANGE SEEDS

"Uncle Julius is back!" my mother said while I was eating breakfast.

"What?" I exclaimed. I didn't believe her. Uncle Julius was a world-famous explorer. He was always traveling to new countries and faraway lands.

Sometimes, he would send me a postcard from the deserts of Mongolia. Or I'd get a letter from the frozen tip of South America.

It had been a year since I had last heard from him. I could hardly believe he was coming to visit.

He was already here! He was at the airport, waiting for my mother to come and pick him up.

My mom was so surprised and excited that she lost her car keys as she was getting ready to pick him up.

She yelled, "Help me find my keys! I just had them!"

I found her keys in their usual place. That was the bottom of her big, black purse.

"Hurry!" she said. We rushed down the stairs, four steps at a time.

She quickly jumped into the car. "Oh no!" she yelled.

"Now what?" I asked.

She turned around and ran back into the apartment building. Then I noticed that she was still wearing her green slippers, the ones decorated with fluffy pink pom-poms.

Finally, after Mom changed her shoes, we made it to the airport. We picked up Uncle Julius. Then we packed his seven suitcases into the car. Finally, we drove home.

An hour later, he was sitting in our living room. He was drinking coffee and telling us about his adventures.

"I crossed the Amazon Rainforest driving an old truck," he said. "It took me three weeks."

"Wow," I said.

Uncle Julius went on, "When I got back to Buenos Aires with my seeds, I hopped on a plane. And here I am!"

"So all of those suitcases are full of seeds?" asked my mom.

Uncle Julius smiled and nodded. "Not just any kind of seeds," he told us. "Some of them are Galaparso seeds!"

"What are Galaparso seeds?" I asked him.

Uncle Julius grinned. He said, "Galaparso trees are very rare and only grow in South America. They grow about as tall as an adult man." He paused, still smiling. Then he went on, "Medicine companies buy the seeds. They use them to make cures for diseases. Each seed is worth a fortune! That's why I'm here. To sell my seeds. Then I have to go to Indonesia in two weeks."

For the last hour, I had been amazed by Uncle Julius's stories. I already knew that I would need more than two weeks to hear about all his adventures.

"Where's Indonesia?" I asked.

Uncle Julius put down his coffee cup. He said, "It's in southeast Asia. I'm going to explore the jungles over there!"

That sounded like so much fun to me. I would love to explore the jungle!

Uncle Julius talked about faraway places like it was no big deal. As if he were talking about walking over to the next street. Uncle Julius's neighborhood was Planet Earth!

Now Uncle Julius looked serious. "The thing is, I need to keep the Galaparso seeds in a cool place until it's time for me to leave," he told us. "It's very important that they stay cool."

My mom looked nervous. "Are they poisonous?" she asked.

Uncle Julius laughed. "Of course not! They simply need to be kept away from light and heat. Otherwise, uh, something could happen," he explained.

"Something?" asked my mom. "What do you mean, something?"

Uncle Julius turned off the living room light. Then he opened one of his suitcases. He pulled out a wooden box from the suitcase.

He opened the box in the dark. A weird green glow filled the room.

"Come look, Sam! Here are the Galaparso seeds!" he whispered excitedly.

About thirty brown seeds were packed at the bottom of my uncle's box. They didn't look special to me. They looked like the nuts you see in the health food section of a grocery store.

The only thing that was interesting about them was the way that they glowed.

Uncle Julius gently placed the box in my hands. Then the glow went away.

He whispered, "Sam, they are now in your care. Go put them in the refrigerator! And please, Sam, be very careful with them."

"Of course," I promised.

And everything that happened afterward was not really my fault.

Chapter 2

THE DANGEROUS SNACK

Lionel had just escaped from the jungle without losing a life. He was entering the Maze of the Living Dead.

I was sprawled on the carpet next to him, holding onto my own videogame controller. I just needed to wait for Lionel to make a mistake. Once he did, I could catch up with him.

"So, where is your famous uncle now?" Lionel asked.

Two zombies on the TV screen were about to attack him with poison arrows. Lionel moved his controller and was safe.

I sighed. At this rate, it was never going to be my turn! I rested my head on my arms. "He had meetings," I said. "He'll be back later. So, are you about to lose?"

It was Wednesday after school. Lionel came over after school to hang out. His videogame player was broken, so he came over to play mine. But that wasn't the only reason he was at my house. My mom works late on Wednesday. She likes me to have someone over to keep me company.

Also, *Total Chaos* is way more fun when you play it with two people. Except when Lionel is always winning.

The evil zombies finally got the best of him. He lost one life point. Finally! It was my turn to fight the evil monsters of *Total Chaos*.

"Whatever. I had cramps in my fingers anyway," he said.

He stood up and clapped his hands together. "Should we eat something? Zombies make me hungry!" he exclaimed.

"Gross," I said. "You can eat, but I want to play the game. I've been waiting to fight zombies for hours!"

Lionel smiled. "If it's okay, I'll make myself a bowl of cereal. All right?" he asked.

"Sure," I said. "There's some candy and cake on the counter too. Take whatever you want. When you come back, I'll be caught up to you for sure!"

Lionel walked out of the living room. "In your dreams!" he yelled from the hallway.

A few minutes later, Lionel came back to the living room with a plate full of goodies. I was busy attacking the zombies.

"This candy is good," Lionel said.

I could hear him shoving handfuls of small candy pieces into his mouth and chomping on them.

I was too busy playing the game to look up at him. I kept fighting zombies.

"Is it peanut butter flavored?" he asked.

"You're the one eating it," I said, killing another zombie.

I was really busy trying to avoid all of the rocks that the zombies were throwing at my head. I didn't have time to look at my friend. In fact, I wasn't really paying attention to him!

"Didn't you look in the bag when you got the candy out of the cupboard?" I asked.

"I didn't get them out of the cupboard," Lionel said. "I found them in the fridge. They're pretty good. A little hard to chew on, but delicious."

I screamed and dropped the controller. "In the fridge?" I yelled.

"Whoa!" Lionel said. "Calm down. I saved some for you."

I was afraid to look. Finally, I turned around.

Lionel had a huge smile on his face. He was pointing to the open box of Galaparso seeds.

Lionel hadn't been eating candy. He'd been eating Galaparso seeds!

My uncle Julius's rare, expensive, important seeds! I couldn't believe it!

"You ate them?" I asked. I didn't scream. My voice sounded like one of the zombies from the videogame.

Lionel started to look a little worried. He frowned and looked down at the box.

"I only ate two or three," he said quickly. "Stop whining. There are plenty left. Hey, what's wrong? I mean, look at your face. You look sick!"

He shoved the box at me.

"Well, I have a reason to be sick!" I yelled.

Then I was quiet. My eyes grew wide. Because right in front of me, something horrible was happening.

Lionel, my best friend, the person who I hung around with all the time, was turning a strange and horrible color.

Lionel was turning green.

Chapter 3

THE TRANSFORMER

Fifteen minutes later, Lionel's face, arms, and hands had all turned light green. His neck was darker green. He sort of looked like a piece of broccoli.

"What's happening to me?" he screamed in a high-pitched voice.

"I don't know!" I yelled. "I don't know what's happening, and I don't know what to do about it!"

I was freaking out!

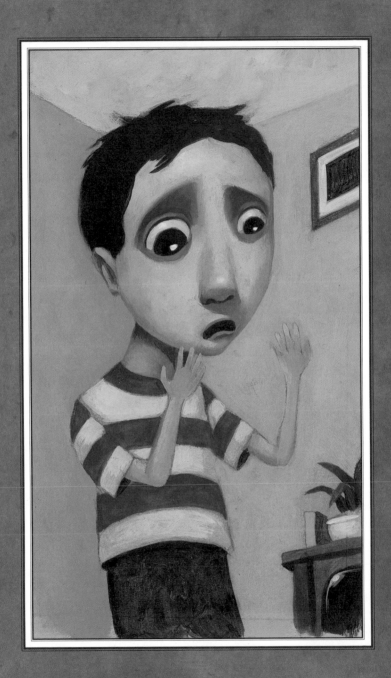

I thought quickly. "How many seeds did you eat?" I asked him.

"Only five or six!" Lionel said in a shaking voice. "I swear! No more than ten, for sure. What kind of candy is that, anyway?"

I sighed. "Those things aren't candy, Lionel," I told him. "They're rare seeds."

Lionel looked really scared. "Sam, do something!" he yelled.

What are you supposed to do when your best friend looks like a piece of broccoli? I would have laughed if I wasn't so scared.

"Okay, try to calm down," I said. "We'll think of something."

I took a deep breath and looked at him.

"Maybe you should take your shirt off so we can see what's going on," I suggested.

Lionel looked like he was going to have a heart attack, but he pulled his T-shirt off over his head.

I had expected to see green all over him, but what I saw was even worse than I had imagined.

Lionel's face was green, all right. But his chest and his stomach were brown.

He wasn't the color of a leaf. It was more like the color of a tree trunk.

I took a deep breath and tried to stay calm.

Lionel pulled up the leg of his pants. His legs were brown too!

He looked at his skin. Then he looked at me. He seemed really scared.

I tried to yell, but only a whisper came out. "Don't move," I croaked. "I'm calling the hospital!"

"What's happening to me, Sam?" Lionel asked again. His voice shook.

"You just ate ten seeds that my uncle brought back from South America!" I replied.

Lionel moaned.

Then I noticed something else. I screamed, "You're sprouting, Lionel!"

"What?" Lionel yelled. "What do you mean, I'm sprouting?"

I couldn't speak. I just pointed to Lionel's shoulder and neck.

A small green branch was poking up.

Lionel was standing there, sprouting leaves and branches, right in my living room. As I watched, another leaf uncurled.

Lionel was shaking with fear. All he could do was stare at me. He looked terrified.

I couldn't tell him that I was just as scared. That would make him feel even worse.

I took a deep breath and calmed myself down. Or pretended to be calm, anyway.

"Does it hurt?" I asked.

"No," Lionel said. "I hardly feel it at all. But Sam, I'm really, really scared. And I'm also very thirsty!"

I thought for a second. I knew my mom usually bought a carton of orange juice when she went to the store. There had to be some in the refrigerator.

"Stay right here. I'll get you some juice," I said.

Lionel shook his head. "No," he said. "Just water! A big bottle of water!"

Quickly, I ran into the kitchen. I found some bottles of water in the fridge.

I grabbed all of them. Then I ran back to the living room.

When I got back, Lionel was looking out the window. He was standing in the sunlight.

When he turned back toward me, my heart almost stopped.

There were leaves in his hair! I could see three of them. They were still small, and shaped like leaves from the tree in front of my apartment building.

As I stood and watched, two more leaves popped out of his head.

Lionel grabbed a bottle of water with his green arms. He drank it really fast. It was gone in a few seconds!

"Quick, I need another one!" he gasped.

Lionel drank up every bottle of water in the house. He must have gone through eight gallons of water before he finally stopped.

Leaves were covering his whole head. On the back of his neck, the little branch had started getting bigger and bigger. It was about ten inches above his head when I decided this whole thing had gone far enough.

"You know what? I really need to call the hospital," I said.

Lionel said, "All right. I'll just stand here by the window. The sun feels great!"

I rushed into my mom's bedroom and called the hospital. She kept the number written down on a piece of paper by the phone.

I dialed the number ten times, and ten times I heard a recording say that all the lines were busy. I couldn't believe it. I felt like I was having a nightmare!

I finally decided that Lionel and I should just go to the hospital. But when I walked back into the living room, I screamed.

Lionel did not need the hospital. He needed his own gardener!

A tree, with dozens of branches going in all directions, was standing in the living room.

The tree turned toward me, crying. It asked, "Is the ambulance coming? Did you tell them to hurry?"

"Uh, they didn't believe me," I lied. "Let's take a taxi!"

That's when I noticed the roots. They were coming out of Lionel's socks and running along the floor. They had dug a hole in the living room rug.

My mom was going to kill me!

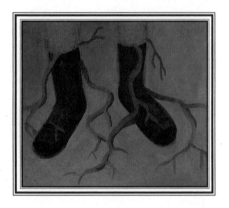

Chapter 4

AN AMAZING RIDE

Riding my bike and carrying Lionel, while he was turning into a tree, was not easy. I knew it was the only way we were going to get him to the hospital.

He couldn't walk, and he was too big to fit into a taxi. Plus, what taxi driver would pick up a kid who was carrying a tree with a face?

Taking my bike was the only choice.

Before I got on the bike, I tied him on with a bunch of ropes. I had to be really careful when I folded his roots. Otherwise, they could get caught in the wheels of my bike.

"Sam, stop it!" Lionel shouted. "You're hurting my roots!"

Luckily, his body was still flexible. He put his hand — or, I mean, his branch — on my shoulder. "You know what, Sam?" Lionel said.

I looked into the tree's face. "I know. You're scared," I said, trying not to sound worried.

Lionel shook his branches. Then he said, "No. What I was going to say was that I've never felt this tall and strong before."

"Just make sure you don't fall off," I said.

I hopped onto the seat of my bike. Then I rode down the street. I could hear Lionel whistling behind me. He sounded happy and calm. "I'm glad you're not freaking out about all this," I said.

Everyone we passed looked twice at us, wondering what was going on. I knew we looked really weird. But I just had to keep pedaling.

To get to the hospital, we had to cross the river. Right before the river, there was a very steep hill. I was worried that Lionel would be nervous while we went downhill. We picked up speed.

"This breeze is great! I can feel it through my leaves!" shouted Lionel.

"You better enjoy it now!" I told him. "It will be a different story after we cross the river. It's going to be all uphill on the other side."

Lionel said, "Sam, I have to dip my roots in the river. I'm thirsty again! I don't feel so good."

I agreed to stop. I was really tired anyway.

I untangled Lionel from my bike. Then I helped him walk over to the shore.

Lionel was looking more and more like a tree. His trunk was darker and thicker and he had more leaves. His face barely showed between his two main branches.

Surprisingly, he seemed calm. He placed his roots in the water and sighed.

"This is great. I was so thirsty," he said.

"Don't drink too much," I told him. "You'll weigh more."

Lionel smiled. He said, "I hope they can help me at the emergency room. I have to admit, it is pretty nice being a tree."

He paused. "It's going to rain," he said.

I laughed. "No way. The sky is clear!" I said. "It is not going to rain."

Lionel frowned. "I'm pretty sure it is," he said.

We looked up at the bright blue sky.

"Will your mom be mad when she sees her rug?" Lionel asked. "And what about your uncle, when he sees that some of the seeds are gone?"

I slapped my forehead. "Oh no! We forgot to put them back in the refrigerator! I have to go back and put the seeds away before it's too late," I said. "I'll be right back!"

"No problem," Lionel said. "I like it here. I could stay here forever."

As I climbed onto my bike, I saw a robin land on Lionel's head. He couldn't wave it away, because his arms were branches.

I rode home as fast as I could.

Chapter 5

ESCAPE FROM THE TREE

My uncle Julius was kneeling on the living room rug, looking into the half-empty box of Galaparso seeds.

My uncle kept repeating, "That's simply incredible! That's just absolutely incredible!"

I took a deep breath. Then I said, "I'm sorry, Uncle Julius. I can explain everything."

Uncle Julius turned around when he heard me. I could see that he had tears in his eyes.

I tried to explain. "It was a mistake," I told him. "Lionel came over, and he didn't know about the Galaparsos."

Uncle Julius interrupted me. "Do you realize what's happening?" he asked.

I sighed. "I know," I said quietly. "It's terrible. I'm so sorry. I left Lionel next to the river."

"Terrible?" Uncle Julius shouted. "The Galaparso seeds started sprouting by themselves. Look!" He held out the box for me to see.

I looked inside the box. Each seed had split and let out a little leaf. The leaves were shaped like tiny blades of grass.

I could see that some drops of water had spilled on the seeds.

"I know," I said quietly. "It's really terrible."

Uncle Julius shook his head. "Terrible? No! You must be joking. It's fantastic!" he cried happily. "They sprouted on their own! It happened so quickly. It's amazing!"

"Do you think it was the bottled water?" I whispered, uncertain.

I thought my uncle would be really mad, but he wasn't. In fact, he looked like he was going to start jumping for joy.

"These Galaparsos are endangered," he told me. "There are only ten trees left on Earth. Can you imagine? These seedlings are a treasure, Sam! They'll be worth millions!"

"Uncle Julius," I said, "I can show you a huge Galaparso tree. And we don't need to wait for years or cross an ocean. It's just five minutes away, next to the river."

Uncle Julius practically pushed me into the car. While we were driving to the river, I told him the whole story. He was very excited to see Lionel, he told me.

We arrived at the river quickly. The tree was right where I had left it, but there wasn't any trace of Lionel.

The Galaparso tree seemed to have stopped growing. Other birds had joined the robin on its branches.

"Wonderful!" my uncle yelled. He jumped out of the car and ran toward the tree. I followed him.

"Lionel! Lionel!" I shouted.

At first, it was kind of funny when Lionel started changing into a tree. It wasn't funny anymore. It was awful to see that the tree didn't have Lionel's face anymore. The trunk and the branches had swallowed up my friend forever.

"Oh no!" I said. "He's gone! He's really gone!"

Uncle Julius patted the tree's bark. "No, it is perfectly healthy," he said, smiling. "I've never seen such a beautiful Galaparso tree!"

"Not the tree," I yelled. "I'm talking about Lionel!"

I picked up some rocks and angrily threw them at the tree's trunk. I was so mad at that stupid Galaparso tree.

"Stop it, Sam!" Uncle Julius shouted.

"Ouch, that hurts!" the tree yelled. "Why don't you find a way to pull me out of here instead of throwing rocks?" it added.

"Lionel?" I whispered.

Uncle Julius and I stared at the tree with our mouths wide open.

"I don't know how it happened," the tree went on, "but the tree stopped being part of me. It started growing around me. It's hollow in here, and I'm trapped. Hurry! It's really hot in here."

I stared at my uncle. "We have to cut the tree open," I told him.

Uncle Julius shook his head. "Are you crazy? This is the world's rarest tree! We can't open it."

"We have to," I said. "Lionel is worth more than an entire Galaparso forest!"

I ran to the car, opened the trunk, and found a screwdriver. Then I started to dig a hole in the bark of the tree.

"Careful!" said Lionel.

"Wait!" Uncle Julius said.

Then Uncle Julius looked through the hole in the trunk.

He saw Lionel's eye.

"Okay," he said finally. "Let's do it."

Uncle Julius and I worked hard. Finally, the opening was large enough to let Lionel get out.

Lionel carefully climbed out from inside the tree.

I was so happy to see him. It was like he had just returned from a long vacation.

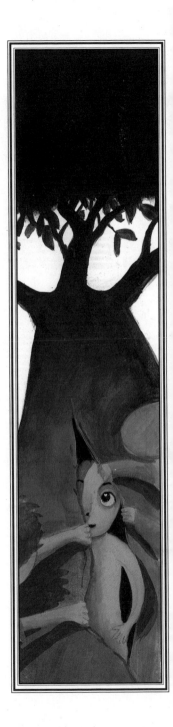